The Desert
of Stolen Dreams

The Desert
of Stolen Dreams

by

Robert Silverberg

Illustrations by Stephen E. Fabian

UNDERWOOD-MILLER
San Francisco, California
Columbia, Pennsylvania
1981

THE DESERT OF STOLEN DREAMS

Signed edition: ISBN 0-934438-44-7
Trade edition: ISBN 0-934438-45-5

Copyright © 1981 by Robert Silverberg
Illustrations copyright © 1981 by Stephen E. Fabian

An Underwood/Miller Book by arrangement with the author. All rights reserved. No part of this book may be reproduced in any form or by any electronic or mechanical means including information storage and retrieval systems without explicit permission from the Author or the Author's agent, except by a reviewer who may quote brief passages. For information address the publisher.

Printed in the United States of America
All Rights Reserved

FIRST EDITION

ILLUSTRATIONS

When he perceived the loving countenance of the
    Lady of the Isle, a deep and powerful bliss
    invaded his soul............................*cover*

Golator Lasgia shook her head. "There is no city
    here, my love."........................*endpapers*

The steetmoy burst forth unexpectedly from the
    darkest part of the woods................*frontispiece*

The floater was passing through a region of dry
    lakebeds....................................*page 8*

As they entered the broad harbor Dekkeret was
    struck by the strangeness of the place.........*page 10*

Her dark tightly coiled hair emitted a surprising
    fragrance..................................*page 26*

Barjazid was a lean and disreputable-looking man..*page 39*

With him were three companions................*page 44*

A long-extinct river swerved in long easy bends
    between the cracked and sundered rock heaps..*page 52*

Dekkeret was stunned by what lay before him......*page 60*

He was naked and there were ants crawling on him. *page 69*

It was the most intense pain he had ever known. . . . *page 85*

The first to rule in Suvrael with the title of King of
    Dreams................................*page 96*

The Desert
of Stolen Dreams

I

SUVRAEL LAY like a glowing sword across the southern horizon—an iron band of dull red light, sending shimmering heat-pulsations into the air. Dekkeret, standing at the bow of the freighter on which he had made the long dreary sea journey, felt a quickening of the pulse. Suvrael at last! That dreadful place, that abomination of a continent, that useless and miserable land, now just a few days away, and who knew what horrors would befall him there? But he was prepared. Whatever happens, Dekkeret believed, happens for the best, in Suvrael as on Castle Mount. He was in his twentieth year, a big burly man with a short neck and enormously broad shoulders. This was the second summer of Lord Prestimion's glorious reign under the great Pontifex Confalume.

It was as an act of penance that Dekkeret had undertaken the voyage to the burning wastes of barren Suvrael. He had committed a shameful deed—certainly not intending it, at first barely realizing the shame of it—while hunting in the Khyntor Marches of the far northland, and some sort of expiation seemed necessary to him. That was in a way a romantic and flamboyant gesture, he knew, but he could forgive himself that. If he did not make romantic and flamboyant gestures at twenty, then when? Surely not ten or fifteen years from now, when he was bound to the wheel of his destinies and had settled snugly in for the inevitable bland easy career in Lord Prestimion's entourage. This was the moment, if ever. So, then, to Suvrael to purge his soul, no matter the consequences.

His friend and mentor and hunting companion in Khyntor, Akbalik, had not been able to understand. But of course Akbalik was no romantic, and a long way beyond twenty, besides. One night in early spring, over a few flasks of hot golden wine in a rough mountain tavern, Dekkeret had announced his intention and Akbalik's response had been a blunt snorting laugh. "Suvrael?" he had cried. "You judge yourself too harshly. There's no sin so foul that it merits a jaunt in Suvrael."

And Dekkeret, stung, feeling patronized, had slowly shaken his head. "Wrongness lies on me like a stain. I'll burn it from my soul under the hotland sun."

"Make the pilgrimage to the Isle instead, if you think you need to do something. Let the blessed Lady heal your spirit."

"No. Suvrael."

"Why?"

"To suffer," said Dekkeret. "To take myself far from the delights of Castle Mount, to the least pleasant place on Majipoor, to a dismal desert of fiery winds and loathsome dangers. To mortify the flesh, Akbalik, and show my contrition. To lay upon myself the discipline of discomfort and even pain—*pain*, do you know what that is?—until I can forgive myself. All right?"

Akbalik, grinning, dug his fingers into the thick robe

of heavy black Khyntor furs that Dekkeret wore. "All right. But if you must mortify, mortify thoroughly. I assume you'll not take this from your body all the while you're under the Suvraelu sun."

Dekkeret chuckled. "There are limits," he said, "to my need for discomfort." He reached for the wine. Akbalik was nearly twice Dekkeret's age, and doubtless found his earnestness funny. So did Dekkeret, to a degree; but that did not swerve him.

"May I try once more to dissuade you?"

"Pointless."

"Consider the waste," said Akbalik anyway. "You have a career to look after. Your name is frequently heard at the Castle now. Lord Prestimion has said high things of you. A promising young man, due to climb far, great strength of character, all that kind of noise. Prestimion's young; he'll rule a long while; those who are young in his early days will rise as he rises. And here you are, deep in the wilds of Khyntor playing when you should be at court, and already planning another and more reckless trip. Forget this Suvrael nonsense, Dekkeret, and return to the Mount with me. Do the Coronal's bidding, impress the great ones with your worth, and build for the future. These are wonderful times on Majipoor, and it will be splendid to be among the wielders of power as things unfold. Eh? Eh? Why throw yourself away in Suvrael? No one knows of this—ah—*sin* of yours, this one little lapse from grace—"

"I know."

"Then promise never to do it again, and absolve yourself."

"It's not so simple," Dekkeret said.

"To squander a year or two of your life, or perhaps lose your life entirely, on a meaningless, useless journey to—"

"Not meaningless. Not useless."

"Except on a purely personal level it is."

"Not so, Akbalik. I've been in touch with the people of the Pontificate and I've wangled an official appointment. I'm a mission of inquiry. Doesn't that sound grand? Suvrael isn't exporting its quota of meat and livestock and the Pontifex wants to know why. You see? I continue to further my career even while going off on what seems to you a wholly private adventure."

"So you've already made arrangements."

"I leave on Fourday next." Dekkeret reached his hand toward his friend. "It'll be at least two years. We'll meet again on the Mount. What do you say, Akbalik, the games at High Morpin, two years from Winterday?"

Akbalik's calm gray eyes fastened intently on Dekkeret's. "I will be there," he said slowly. "I pray that you'll be too."

That conversation lay only some months in the past; but to Dekkeret now, feeling the throbbing heat of the southern continent reaching toward him over the pale green water of the Inner Sea, it seemed incredibly long ago, and the voyage infinitely long. The first part of the journey had been pleasing enough—down out of the mountains to the grand metropolis of Ni-moya, and then by riverboat down the Zimr to the port of Piliplok on the eastern coast. There he had boarded a freighter, the cheapest transport he could find, bound for the Suvraelu city of Tolaghai, and then it had been south

THE DESERT OF STOLEN DREAMS

and south and south all summer long, in a ghastly little cabin just downwind from a hold stuffed with bales of dried baby sea-dragons, and as the ship crossed into the tropics the days presented a heat unlike anything he had ever known, and the nights were little better; and the crew, mostly a bunch of shaggy Skandars, laughed at his discomfort and told him he had better enjoy the cool weather while he could, for real heat was waiting for him in Suvrael. Well, he had wanted to suffer, and his wish was being amply granted already, and worse to come. He did not complain. He felt no regret. But his comfortable life among the young knights of Castle Mount had not prepared him for sleepless nights with the reek of sea-dragon in his nostrils like stilettos, nor for the stifling heat that engulfed the ship a few weeks out of Piliplok, nor for the intense boredom of the unchanging seascape. The planet was so impossibly *huge*, that was the trouble. It took forever to get from anywhere to anywhere. Crossing from his native continent of Alhanroel to the western land of Zimroel had been a big enough project, overland to Alaisor from the Mount, then by sea to Piliplok and up the river into the mountain marches, but he had Akbalik with him to lighten the time, and there had been the excitement of his first major journey, the strangeness of new places, new foods, new accents. And he had had the hunting expedition to look forward to. But this? This imprisonment aboard a dirty creaking ship stuffed with parched meat of evil odor? This interminable round of empty days without friends, without duties, without conversation? If only some monstrous sea-dragon would heave into view, he thought, and enliven the journey with a bit of peril; but no, no, the dragons in their migrations were elsewhere, one great herd said to be in western waters out by Narabal just now and another midway between Piliplok and the Rodamaunt Archipelago, and Dekkeret saw none of the vast beasts, not even a few stragglers. What made the boredom worse was that it did not seem to have any value as catharsis. He was suffering, true, and suffering was what he imagined would heal him of his wound, but yet the awareness of the terrible thing he had done in the mountains did not seem to diminish at all. He was hot and bored and restless, and guilt still clawed at him, and still he tormented himself with the ironic knowledge that he was being praised by no less than the Coronal Lord Prestimion for great strength of character while he could find only weakness and cowardice and foolishness in himself. Perhaps it takes more than humidity and boredom and foul odors to cure one's soul, Dekkeret decided. At any rate he had had more than enough of the process of getting to Suvrael, and he was ready to begin the next phase of his pilgrimage into the unknown.

II

VERY JOURNEY ENDS, even an endless one. The hot wind out of the south intensified day after day until the deck was too hot to walk and the barefoot Skandars had to swab it down every few hours; and then suddenly the burning mass of sullen darkness on the horizon resolved itself into a shoreline and the jaws of a harbor. They had reached Tolaghai at last.

All of Suvrael was tropical; most of its interior was desert, oppressed perpetually by a colossal weight of dry dead air around the periphery of which searing cyclones whirled; but the fringes of the continent were more or less habitable, and there were five major cities along the coasts, of which Tolaghai was the largest and the one most closely linked by commerce to the rest of Majipoor. As the freighter entered the broad harbor Dekkeret was struck by the strangeness of the place. In his brief time he had seen a great many of the giant world's cities—a dozen of the fifty on the flanks of Castle Mount, and towering windswept Alaisor, and the vast astounding white-walled Ni-moya, and magnificent Piliplok, and many others—and never had he beheld a city with the harsh, mysterious, forbidding look of this one. Tolaghai clung like a crab to a low ridge along the sea. Its buildings were flat, squat things of sun-dried orange brick, with mere slits for windows, and there were only sparse plantings around them, dismaying angular palms, mainly, that were all bare trunk with tiny feathery crowns far overhead. Here at midday the streets were almost deserted. The hot wind blew sprays of sand over the cracked paving-stones. To Dekkeret the city seemed like some sort of prison outpost, brutal and ugly, or perhaps a city out of time, belonging to some prehistoric folk of a regimented and authoritarian race. Why had anyone chosen to build a place so hideous? Doubtless it was out of mere efficiency, ugliness like this being the best way to cope with the climate of the land, but still, still, Dekkeret thought, the challenges of heat and drought might surely have called forth some less repellent architecture.

In his innocence Dekkeret thought he could simply go ashore at once, but that was not how things worked here. The ship lay at anchor for more than an hour before the port officials, three glum-looking Hjorts, came aboard. Then followed a lengthy business with sanitary inspections and cargo manifests and haggling over docking fees; and finally the dozen or so passengers were cleared for landing. A porter of the Ghayrog race seized Dekkeret's luggage and asked the name of his hotel. He replied that he had not booked one, and the reptilian-looking creature, tongue flickering and black fleshy hair writhing like a mass of serpents, gave him an icy look and said, "What will you pay? Are you rich?"

"Not very. What can I get for three crowns a night?"
"Little. Bed of straw. Vermin on the walls."
"Take me there," said Dekkeret.

THE DESERT OF STOLEN DREAMS

The Ghayrog looked as startled as a Ghayrog is capable of looking. "You will not be happy there, fine sir. You have the bearing of lordship about you."

"Perhaps so, but I have a poor man's purse. I'll take my chances with the vermin."

Actually the inn turned out to be not as bad as he feared: ancient, squalid, and depressing, yes, but so was everything else in sight, and the room he received seemed almost palatial after his lodgings on the ship. Nor was there the reek of sea-dragon flesh here, only the arid piercing flavor of Suvraelu air, like the stuff within a flask that had been sealed a thousand years. He gave the Ghayrog a half-crown piece, for which he had no thanks, and unpacked his few belongings.

In late afternoon Dekkeret went out. The stifling heat had dropped not at all, but the thin cutting wind seemed less fierce now, and there were more people in the streets. All the same the city felt grim. This was the right sort of place for doing a penance. He loathed the blank-faced brick buildings, he hated the withered look of the landscape, and he missed the soft sweet air of his native city of Normork on the lower slopes of Castle Mount. Why, he wondered, would anyone choose to live here, when there was opportunity aplenty on the gentler continents? What starkness of the soul drove some millions of his fellow citizens to scourge themselves in the daily severities of life on Suvrael?

The representatives of the Pontificate had their offices on the great blank plaza fronting the harbor. Dekkeret's instructions called upon him to present himself there, and despite the lateness of the hour he found the place open, for in the searing heat all citizens of Tolaghai observed a midday closing and transacted business well into the evening. He was left to wait a while in an antechamber decorated with huge white ceramic portraits of the reigning monarchs, the Pontifex Confalume shown in full face with a look of benign but overwhelming grandeur, and young Lord Prestimion the Coronal in profile, eyes aglitter, with intelligence and dynamic energy. Majipoor was fortunate in her rulers, Dekkeret thought. When he was a boy he had seen Confalume, then Coronal, holding court in the wondrous city of Bombifale high up the Mount, and he had wanted to cry out from sheer joy at the man's calmness and radiant strength. A few years later Lord Confalume succeeded to the Pontificate and went to dwell in the subterranean recesses of the Labyrinth, and Prestimion had been made Coronal—a very different man, equally impressive but all dash and vigor and impulsive power. It was while Lord Prestimion was making the grand processional through the cities of the Mount that he had spied young Dekkeret in Normork and had chosen him, in his random unpredictable way, to join the knights in training in the High Cities. Which seemed an epoch ago, such great changes having occurred in Dekkeret's life since then. At eighteen he had allowed himself fantasies of ascending the Coronal's throne himself one day; but then had come his ill-starred holiday in the mountains of Zimroel, and now, scarcely past twenty, fidgeting in a dusty outer office in this drab city of cheerless Suvrael, he felt he had no future at all, only a barren stretch of meaningless years to use up.

A pudgy sour-faced Hjort appeared and announced,

THE DESERT OF STOLEN DREAMS

"The Archiregimand Golator Lasgia will see you now."

That was a resonant title; but its owner proved to be a slender dark-skinned woman not greatly older than Dekkeret, who gave him careful scrutiny out of large glossy solemn eyes. In a perfunctory way she offered him greeting with the hand-symbol of the Pontificate and took the document of his credentials from him. "The Initiate Dekkeret," she murmured. "Mission of inquiry, under the commission of the Khyntor provincial superstrate. I don't understand, Initiate Dekkeret. Do you serve the Coronal or the Pontifex?"

Uncomfortably Dekkeret said, "I am of Lord Prestimion's staff, a very low echelon. But while I was in Khyntor Province a need arose at the office of the Pontificate for an investigation of certain things in Suvrael, and when the local officials discovered that I was bound for Suvrael anyway, they asked me in the interests of economy to take on the job even though I was not in the employ of the Pontifex. And—"

Tapping Dekkeret's papers thoughtfully against her desktop, Golator Lasgia said, "You were bound for Suvrael anyway? May I ask why?"

Dekkeret flushed. "A personal matter, if you please."

She let it pass. "And what affairs of Suvrael can be of such compelling interest to my pontifical brothers of Khyntor, or is my curiosity on that subject also misplaced?"

Dekkeret's discomfort grew. "It has to do with an imbalance of trade," he answered, barely able to meet her cool penetrating gaze. "Khyntor is a manufacturing center; it exchanges goods for the livestock of Suvrael; for the past two years the export of blaves and mounts out of Suvrael has declined steadily, and now strains are developing in the Khyntor economy. The manufacturers are encountering difficulty in carrying so much Suvraelu credit.'

"None of this is news to me."

"I've been asked to inspect the rangelands here," said Dekkeret, "in order to determine whether an upturn in livestock production can soon be expected."

"Will you have some wine?' Golator Lasgia asked unexpectedly.

Dekkeret, adrift, considered the proprieties. While he faltered she produced two flasks of golden, deftly snapped their seals, and passed one to him. He took it with a grateful smile. The wine was cold, sweet, with a faint sparkle.

"Wine of Khyntor," she said. "Thus we contribute to the Suvraelu trade deficit. The answer, Initiate Dekkeret, is that in the final year of the Pontifex Prankipin a terrible drought struck Suvrael—you may ask, Initiate, how we can tell the difference here between a year of drought and a year of normal rainfall, but there is a difference, Initiate, there is a significant difference —and the grazing districts suffered. There was no way of feeding our cattle, so we butchered as many as the market could hold, and sold much of the remaining stock to ranchers in western Zimroel. Not long after Confalume succeeded to the Labyrinth, the rains returned and the grass began to grow in our savannas. But it takes several years to rebuild the herds. Therefore the trade imbalance will continue a time longer, and then will be cured." She smiled without warmth. "There. I have spared you the inconvenience of an uninteresting journey to the interior."

Dekkeret found himself perspiring heavily. "Nevertheless I must make it, Archregimand Golator Lasgia."

"You'll learn nothing more than I've just told you."

"I mean no disrespect. But my commission specifically requires me to see with my own eyes—"

She closed hers a moment. "To reach the rangelands just now will involve you in great difficulties, extreme physical discomfort, perhaps considerable personal danger. If I were you, I'd remain in Tolaghai, sampling such pleasures as are available here, and dealing with whatever personal business brought you to Suvrael; and after a proper interval, write your report in consultation with my office and take yourself back to Khyntor."

Immediate suspicions blossomed in Dekkeret. The branch of the government she served was not always cooperative with the Coronal's people; she seemed quite transparently trying to conceal something that was going on in Suvrael; and, although his mission of inquiry was only the pretext for his voyage to this place and not his central task, all the same he had his career to consider, and if he allowed a Pontifical Archregimand to bamboozle him too easily here it would go badly for him later. He wished he had not accepted the wine from her. But to cover his confusion he allowed himself a series of suave sips, and at length said, "My sense of honor would not permit me to follow such an easy course."

"How old are you, Initiate Dekkeret?"

"I was born in the twelfth year of Lord Confalume."

"Yes, your sense of honor would still prick you, then. Come, look at this map with me." She rose briskly. She was taller than he expected, nearly his own height, which gave her a fragile appearance. Her dark, tightly coiled hair emitted a surprising fragrance, even over the aroma of the strong wine. Golator Lasgia touched the wall and a map of Suvrael in brilliant ochre and auburn hues sprang into view. "This is Tolaghai," she said, tapping the northwest corner of the continent. "The grazing lands are here." She indicated a band that began six or seven hundred miles inland and ran in a rough circle surrounding thedesert at the heart of Suvrael. "From Tolaghai," she went on, "there are three main routes to the cattle country. This is one. At present it is ravaged by sandstorms and no traffic can safely use it. This is the second route: we are experiencing certain difficulties with Shapeshifter bandits there, and it is also closed to travelers. The third way lies here, by Khulag Pass, but that road has fallen into disuse of late, and an arm of the great desert has begun to encroach on it. Do you see the problems?"

As gently as he could Dekkeret said, "But if it is the business of Suvrael to raise cattle for export, and all the routes between the grazing lands and the chief port are blocked, is it correct to say that a lack of pasture is the true cause of the recent shortfalls of cattle exports?"

She smiled. "There are other ports from which we ship our produce in this current situation."

"Well, then, if I go to one of those, I should find an open highway to the cattle country."

THE DESERT OF STOLEN DREAMS

Again she tapped the map. "Since last winter the port of Natu Gorvinu has been the center of the cattle trade. This is it, in the east, under the coast of Alhanroel, about six thousand miles from here."

"Six thousand—"

"There is little reason for commerce between Tolaghai and Natu Gorvinu. Perhaps once a year a ship goes from one to the other. Overland the situation is worse, for the roads out of Tolaghai are not maintained east of Kangheez—" she indicated a city perhaps a thousand miles away—"and beyond that, who knows? This is not a heavily settled continent."

"Then there's no way to reach Natu Gorvinu?" Dekkeret said, stunned.

"One. By ship from Tolaghai to Stoien on Alhanroel, and from Stoien to Natu Gorvinu. It should take you only a little over a year. By the time you reach Suvrael again and penetrate the interior, of course, the crisis that you've come to investigate will probably be over. Another flask of the golden, Initiate Dekkeret?"

Numbly he accepted the wine. The distances stupefied him. Another horrendous voyage across the Inner Sea, all the way back to his native continent of Alhanroel, only to turn around and cross the water a third time, sailing now to the far side of Suvrael, and then to find, probably, that the ways to the interior had meanwhile been closed out there, and—no. No. There was such a thing as carrying a penance too far. Better to abandon the mission altogether than subject himself to such absurdities. While he hesitated Golator Lasgia said, "The hour is late and your problems need longer consideration. Have you plans for dinner, Initiate Dekkeret?"

Suddenly, astonishingly, her somber eyes gleamed with mischief of a familiar kind.

III

IN THE COMPANY of the Archregimand Golator Lasgia, Dekkeret discovered that life in Tolaghai was not necessarily as bleak as first superficial inspection had indicated. By floater she returned him to his hotel—he could see her distaste at the look of the place—and instructed him to rest and cleanse himself and be ready in an hour. A coppery twilight had descended, and by the time the hour had elapsed the sky was utterly black, with only a few alien constellations cutting jagged tracks across it, and the crescent hint of one or two moons down near the horizon. She called for him punctually. In place of her stark official tunic she wore now something of clinging mesh, almost absurdly seductive. Dekkeret was puzzled by all this. He had had his share of success with women, yes, but so far as he knew he had given her no sign of interest, nothing but the most formal of respect; and yet she clearly was assuming a night of intimacy. Why? Certainly not his irresistible sophistication and physical appeal, nor any political advantage he could confer on her, nor any other rational motive. Except one, that this was a foul backwater outpost where life was stale and uncomfortable, and he was a youthful stranger who might provide a woman herself still young with a night's amusement. He felt used by that, but otherwise he could see no great harm in it. And after months at sea he was willing to run a little risk in the name of pleasure.

They dined at a private club on the outskirts of town, in a garden elegantly decorated with the famous creature-plants of Stoienzar and other flowering wonders that had Dekkeret calculating how much of Tolaghai's modest water supply was diverted toward keeping this one spot flourishing. At other tables, widely separated, were Suvraelinu in handsome costume, and Golator Lasgia nodded to this one and that, but no one approached her, nor did they stare unduly at Dekkeret. From within the building blew a cool refreshing breeze, the first he had felt in weeks, as though some miraculous machine of the ancients, some cousin to the ones that generated the delicious atmosphere of Castle Mount, were at work in there. Dinner was a magnificent affair of lightly fermented fruits and tender juicy slabs of a pale green-fleshed fish, accompanied by a fine dry wine of Amblemorn, no less, the very fringes of Castle Mount. She drank freely, as did he; they grew bright-eyed and animated; the chilly formality of the interview in her office dropped away. He learned that she was nine years his senior, that she was a native of moist lush Narabal on the western continent, that she had entered the service of the Pontifex when still a girl, and had been stationed in Suvrael for the past ten years, rising upon Confalume's accession to the Pontificate to her present high administrative post in Tolaghai.

"Do you *like* it here?" he asked.

She shrugged. "One gets accustomed to it."

"I doubt that I would. To me Suvrael is merely a place of torment, a kind of purgatory."

Golator Lasgia nodded. "Exactly."

There was a flash from her eyes to his. He did not dare ask for amplification; but something told him that they had much in common, that she had not been assigned to this wretched place but had requested service here for some dark secret reason of atonement.

He filled their glasses once again and permitted himself the perils of a calm, knowing smile.

She said, "Is it purgatory you seek here?"

"Yes."

She indicated the lavish gardens, the empty wineflasks, the costly dishes, the half-eaten delicacies. "You have made a poor start, then."

"Milady, dinner with you was no part of my plan."

"Nor mine. But the Divine provides, and we accept. Yes? Yes?" She leaned close. "What will you do now? The voyage to Natu Gorvinu?"

"It seems too heavy an enterprise."

"Then do as I say. Stay in Tolaghai until you grow weary of it; then return and file your report. No one will be the wiser in Khyntor."

"No. I must go inland."

Her expression grew mocking. "Such dedication! But how will you do it? The roads from here are closed."

"You mentioned the one by Khulag Pass, that had fallen into disuse. Mere disuse doesn't seem as serious as deadly sandstorms, or Shapeshifter bandits. Perhaps I can hire a caravan leader to take me that way."

"Into the desert?"

"If needs be."

"The desert is haunted," said Golator Lasgia casually. "You should forget that idea. Call the waiter over: we need more wine."

"I think I've had enough, milady."

"Come, then. We'll go elsewhere."

Stepping from the breeze-cooled garden to the dry hot night air of the street was a shock; but quickly they were in her floater, and not long after they were in a second garden, this one in the courtyard of her official residence, surrounding a pool. There were no weather-machines here to ease the heat, but the Archregimand had another way, dropping her gown and going to the pool. Her lean, supple body gleamed a moment in the starlight; then she dived, sliding nearly without a splash beneath the surface. She beckoned to him and quickly he joined her.

Afterward they embraced on a bed of close-cropped thick-bladed grass. It was almost as much like wrestling as lovemaking, for she clasped him with her long muscular legs, tried to pinion his arms, rolled over and over with him, laughing, and he was amazed at the strength of her, the playful ferocity of her movements. But when they were through testing one another they moved with more harmony, and it was a night of little sleep and much exertion.

Dawn was an amazement: without warning, the sun was in the sky like a trumpet-blast, roasting the surrounding hills with shafts of hot light.

They lay limp, exhausted. Dekkeret turned to her—by cruel morning light she looked less girlish than she had under the stars—and said abruptly, "Tell me about this haunted desert. What spirits will I meet there?"

"How persistent you are!"

"Tell me."

"There are ghosts there that can enter your dreams and steal them. They rob your soul of joy and leave fears in its place. By day they sing in the distance, confusing you, leading you from the path with their clatter and their music."

"Am I supposed to believe this?"

"In recent years many who have entered that desert have perished there."

"Of dream-stealing ghosts."

"So it is said."

"It will make a good tale to tell when I return to Castle Mount, then."

"*If* you return," she said.

"You say that not everyone who has gone into that desert has died of it. Obviously not, for someone has come out to tell the tale. Then I will hire a guide, and take my chances among the ghosts."

"No one will accompany you."

"Then I'll go alone."

"And certainly die." She stroked his powerful arms and made a little purring sound. "Are you so interested in dying, so soon? Dying has no value. It confers no benefits. Whatever peace you seek, the peace of the grave is not it. Forget the desert journey. Stay here with me."

"We'll go together."

She laughed. "I think not."

It was, Dekkeret realized, madness. He had doubts of her tales of ghosts and dream-stealers, unless what went on in that desert was some trickery of the rebellious aborigines of the planet, the Shapeshifters or Metamorphs, and even then he doubted it. Perhaps all her tales of danger were only ruses to keep him longer in Tolaghai. Flattering if true, but of no help in his quest. And she was right about death being a useless form of purgation. If his adventures in Suvrael were to have meaning, he must succeed in surviving them.

Golator Lasgia drew him to his feet. They bathed briefly in the pool; then she led him within, to the most handsomely appointed dwelling he had seen this side of Castle Mount, and gave him a breakfast of fruits and dried fish.

Suddenly in mid-morning she said, "*Must* you go into the interior?"

"An inner need drives me in that direction."

"Very well. We have in Tolaghai a certain scoundrel who often ventures inland by way of Khulag Pass, or so he claims, and seems to survive it. For a purse full of royals he'll no doubt guide you there. His name is Barjazid; and if you insist, I'll summon him and ask him to assist you."

IV

"SCOUNDREL" seemed the proper word for Barjazid. He was a lean and disreputable-looking little man, shabbily dressed in an old brown robe and worn leather sandals, with an ancient necklace of mismatched sea-dragon bones at his throat. His lips were thin, his eyes had a feverish glaze, his skin was burned almost black by the desert sun. He stared at Dekkeret as though weighing the contents of his purse.

"If I take you," said Barjazid in a voice altogether lacking in resonance but yet not weak, "you will first sign a quitclaim absolving me of any responsibility to your heirs, in the event of your death."

"I have no heirs," Dekkeret replied.

"Kinfolk, then. I won't be hauled into the Pontifical courts by your father or your elder sister because you've perished in the desert."

"Have you perished in the desert yet?"

Barjazid looked baffled. "An absurd question."

"You go into that desert," Dekkeret persisted, "and you return alive. Yes? Well then, if you know your trade, you'll come out alive again this time, and so will I. I'll do what you do and go where you go. If you live, I live. If I perish, you'll have perished too, and my family will have no lien."

"I can withstand the power of the stealers of dreams," said Barjazid. This I know from ample tests. How do you know you'll prevail over them as readily?"

Dekkeret helped himself to a new serving of Barjazid's tea, a rich infusion brewed from some potent shrub of the sandhills. The two men squatted on mounds of haigus-hide blankets in the musty back room of a shop belonging to Barjazid's brother's son: it was evidently a large clan. Dekkeret sipped the sharp, bitter tea reflectively and said, after a moment, "Who are these dream-stealers?"

"I cannot say."

"Shapeshifters, perhaps?"

Barjazid shrugged. "They have not bothered to tell me their pedigree. Shapeshifters, Ghayrogs, Vroons, ordinary humans— how would I know? In dreams all voices are alike. Certainly there are tribes of Shapeshifters loose in the desert, and some of them are angry folk given to mischief, and perhaps they have the skill of touching minds along with the skill of altering their bodies. Or perhaps not."

"If the Shapeshifters have closed two of the three routes out of Tolaghai, the Coronal's forces have work to do here."

"This is no affair of mine."

"The Shapeshifters are a subjugated race. They must not be allowed to disrupt the daily flow of life on Majipoor."

"It was you who suggested that the dream-stealers

THE DESERT OF STOLEN DREAMS

were Shapeshifters," Barjazid pointed out acidly. "I myself have no such theory. And who the dream-stealers are is not important. What is important is that they make the lands beyond Khulag Pass dangerous for travelers."

"Why do you go there, then?"

"I am not likely ever to answer a question that begins with *why*," said Barjazid. "I go there because I have reason to go there. Unlike others, I seem to return alive."

"Does everyone else who crosses the pass die?"

"I doubt it. I have no idea. Beyond question many have perished since the dream-stealers first were heard from. At the best of times that desert has been perilous." Barjazid stirred his tea. He began to appear restless. "If you accompany me, I'll protect you as best I can. But I make no guarantees for your safety. Which is why I demand that you give me legal absolution from responsibility."

Dekkeret said, "If I sign such a paper it would be signing a death warrant. What would keep you from murdering me ten miles beyond the pass, robbing my corpse, and blaming it all on the dream-stealers?"

"By the Lady, I am no murderer! I am not even a thief."

"But to give you a paper saying that if I die on the journey you are not to be blamed—might that not tempt even an honest man beyond all limits?"

Barjazid's eyes blazed with fury. He gestured as though to bring the interview to an end. "What goes beyond limits is your audacity," he said, rising and tossing his cup aside. "Find another guide, if you fear me so much."

Dekkeret, remaining seated, said quietly, "I regret the suggestion. I ask you only to see my position: a stranger and a young man in a remote and difficult land, forced to seek the aid of those he does not know to take him into places where improbable things happen. I must be cautious."

"Be even more cautious, then. Take the next ship for Stoien and return to the easy life of Castle Mount."

"I ask you again to guide me. For a good price, and nothing more about signing a quitclaim to my life. How much is your fee?"

"Thirty royals," Barjazid said.

Dekkeret grunted as though he had been struck below the ribs. It had cost him less than that to sail from Piliplok to Tolaghai. Thirty royals was a year's wage for someone like Barjazid; to pay it would require Dekkeret to draw on an expensive letter of credit. His impulse was to respond with knightly scorn, and offer ten; but he realized that he had forfeited his bargaining strength by objecting to the quitclaim. If he haggled now over the price as well, Barjazid would simply terminate the negotiations.

He said at length, "So be it. But no quitclaim."

Barjazid gave him a sour look. "Very well. No quitclaim, as you insist."

"How is the money to be paid?"

"Half now, half on the morning of departure."

"Ten now," said Dekkeret, "and ten on the morning of departure, and ten on the day of my return to Tolaghai."

THE DESERT OF STOLEN DREAMS

"That makes a third of my fee conditional on your surviving the trip. Remember that I make no guarantee of that."

"Perhaps my survival becomes more likely if I hold back a third of the fee until the end."

"One expects a certain haughtiness from one of the Coronal's knights, and one learns to ignore it as a mere mannerism, up to a point. But I think you have passed the point." Once again Barjazid made a gesture of dismissal. "There is too little trust between us. It would be a poor idea for us to travel together."

"I meant no disrespect," said Dekkeret.

"But you ask me to leave myself to the mercies of your kinfolk if you perish, and you seem to regard me as an ordinary cutthroat or at best a brigand, and you feel it necessary to arrange my fee so that I will have less motivation to murder you." Barjazid spat. "The other face of haughtiness is courtesy, young knight. A Skandar dragon-hunter would have shown me more courtesy. I did not seek your employ, bear in mind. I will not humiliate myself to aid you. If you please—"

"Wait."

"I have other business this morning."

"Fifteen royals now," said Dekkeret, "and fifteen royals when we set forth, as you say. Yes?"

"Even though you think I'll murder you in the desert?"

"I became too suspicious because I didn't want to appear too innocent," said Dekkeret. "It was tactless for me to have said the things I said. I ask you to hire yourself to me on the terms agreed."

Barjazid was silent.

From his purse Dekkeret drew three five-royal coins. Two were pieces of the old coinage, showing the Pontifex Prankipin with Lord Confalume. The third was a brilliant newly-minted one, bearing Confalume as Pontifex and the image of Lord Prestimion on the reverse. He extended them toward Barjazid, who selected the new coin and examined it with great curiosity.

"I have not seen one of these before," he said. "Shall we call in my brother's son for an opinion of its authenticity?"

It was too much. "Do you take me for a passer of false money?" Dekkeret roared, leaping to his feet and looming ferociously over the small man. Rage throbbed in him; he came close to striking Barjazid.

But he perceived that the other was altogether fearless and unmoving in the face of his wrath. Barjazid actually smiled, and took the other two coins from Dekkeret's trembling hand.

"So you too have little liking for groundless accusations, eh, young knight?" Barjazid laughed. "Let us have a treaty, then. You'll not expect me to assassinate you beyond Khulag Pass, and I'll not send your coins out to the money-changer's for an appraisal, eh? Well? Is it agreed?"

Dekkeret nodded wearily.

"Nevertheless this is a risky journey," said Barjazid, "and I would not have you too confident of a safe return. Much depends on your strength when the time of testing comes."

"So be it. When do we leave?"

"Fiveday, at the sunset hour. We depart the city from

Pinitor Gate. Is that place known to you?"

"I'll find it," Dekkeret said. "Till Fiveday, at sunset."

He offered the little man his hand.

V

IVEDAY was three days hence. Dekkeret did not regret the delay, for that gave him three more nights with the Archregimand Golator Lasgia; or so he thought, but in fact it happened otherwise. She was not at her office by the waterfront on the evening of Dekkeret's meeting with Barjazid, nor would her aides transmit a message to her. He wandered the torrid city disconsolately until long after dark, finding no companionship at all, and ultimately ate a drab and gritty meal at his hotel, still hoping that Golator Lasgia would miraculously appear and whisk him away. She did not, and he slept fitfully and uneasily, his mind obsessed by the memories of her smooth flanks, her small firm breasts, her hungry, aggressive mouth. Toward dawn came a dream, vague and unreadable, in which she and Barjazid and some Hjorts and Vroons performed a complex dance in a roofless and sand-swept stone ruin, and afterward he fell into a sound sleep, not awakening until midday on Seaday. The entire city appeared to be in hiding then, but when the cooler hours came he went round to the Archregimand's office once again, once again not seeing her, and then spent the evening in the same purposeless fashion as the night before. As he gave himself up to sleep he prayed fervently to the Lady of the Isle to

THE DESERT OF STOLEN DREAMS

send Golator Lasgia to him. But it was not the function of the Lady to do such things, and all that did reach him in the night was a bland and cheering dream, perhaps a gift of the blessed Lady but probably not, in which he dwelled in a thatched hut on the shores of the Great Sea by Til-omon and nibbled on sweet purplish fruits that squirted juice to stain his cheeks. When he awakened he found a Hjort of the Archregimand's staff waiting outside his room, to summon him to the presence of Golator Lasgia.

That evening they dined together late, and went to her villa again, for a night of lovemaking that made their other one seem like a month of chastity. Dekkeret did not ask her at any time why she had refused him these two nights past, but as they breakfasted on spiced gihorna-skin and golden wine, both he and she vigorous and fresh after having had no sleep whatever, she said, "I wish I had had more time with you this week, but at least we were able to share your final night. Now you'll go to the Desert of Stolen Dreams with my taste on your lips. Have I made you forget all other women?"

"You know the answer."

"Good. Good. You may never embrace a woman again; but the last was the best, and few are so lucky as that."

"Were you so certain I'll die in the desert, then?"

"Few travelers return," she said. "The chances of my seeing you again are slight."

Dekkeret shivered faintly—not out of fear, but in recognition of Golator Lasgia's inner motive. Some morbidity in her evidently had led her to snub him those two nights, so that the third would be all the more intense, for she must believe that he would be a dead man shortly after and she wanted the special pleasure of being his last woman. That chilled him. If he were going to die before long, Dekkeret would just as soon have had the other two nights with her as well; but apparently the subtleties of her mind went beyond such crass notions. He bade her a courtly farewell, not knowing if they would meet again or even if he wished it, for all her beauty and voluptuary skills. Too much that was mysterious and dangerously capricious lay coiled within her.

Not long before sunset he presented himself at Pinitor Gate on the city's southeastern flank. It would not have surprised him if Barjazid had reneged on their agreement, but no, a floater was waiting just outside the pitted sandstone arch of the old gate, and the little man stood leaning against the vehicle's side. With him were three companions: a Vroon, a Skandar, and a slender, hard-eyed young man who was obviously Barjazid's son.

At a nod from Barjazid the giant four-armed Skandar took hold of Dekkeret's two sturdy bags and stowed them with a casual flip in the floater's keep. "Her name," said Barjazid, "is Khaymak Gran. She is unable to speak, but far from stupid. She has served me many years, since I found her tongueless and more than half dead in the desert. The Vroon is Serifain Reinaulion, who often speaks too much, but knows the desert tracks better than anyone of this city." Dekkeret exchanged brusque salutes with the small tentacular be-

THE DESERT OF STOLEN DREAMS

ing. "And my son, Dinitak, will also accompany us," Barjazid said. "Are you well rested, Initiate?"

"Well enough," Dekkeret answered. He had slept most of the day, after his unsleeping night.

"We travel mainly by darkness, and camp in the heat of the day. My understanding is that I am to take you through Khulag Pass, across the wasteland known as the Desert of Stolen Dreams, and to the edge of the grazing lands around Ghyzyn Kor, where you have certain inquiries to make among the herdsmen. And then back to Tolaghai. Is this so?"

"Exactly," Dekkeret said.

Barjazid made no move to enter the floater. Dekkeret frowned; and then he understood. From his purse he produced three more five-royal pieces, two of them old ones of the Prankipin coinage, the third a shining coin of Lord Prestimion. These he handed to Barjazid, who plucked forth the Prestimion coin and tossed it to his son. The boy eyed the bright coin suspiciously. "The new Coronal," said Barjazid. "Make yourself familiar with his face. We'll be seeing it often."

"He will have a glorious reign," said Dekkeret. "He will surpass even Lord Confalume in grandeur. Already a wave of new prosperity sweeps the northern continents, and they were prosperous enough before. Lord Prestimion is a man of vigor and decisiveness, and his plans are ambitious."

Barjazid said, with a shrug, "Events on the northern continents carry very little weight here, and somehow prosperity on Alhanroel or Zimroel has a way of mattering hardly at all to Suvrael. But we rejoice that the

Divine has blessed us with another splendid Coronal. May he remember, occasionally, that there is a southern land also, and citizens of his realm dwelling in it. Come, now: time to be traveling."

VI

THE PINITOR GATE marked an absolute boundary between city and desert. To one side there was a district of low sprawling villas, walled and faceless; to the other was only barren waste beyond the city's perimeter. Nothing broke the emptiness of the desert but the highway, a broad cobbled track that wound slowly upward toward the crest of the ridge that encircled Tolaghai.

The heat was intolerable. By night the desert was perceptibly cooler than by day, but scorching all the same. Though the great blazing eye of the sun was gone, the orange sands, radiating the stored heat of the day toward the sky, shimmered and sizzled with the intensity of a banked furnace. A strong wind was blowing—at the coming of the darkness, Dekkeret had noticed, the flow of the wind reversed, blowing now from the heart of the continent toward the sea—but it made no difference: shore-wind or sea-wind, both were oppressive streams of dry baking air that offered no mercies.

In the clear arid atmosphere the light of the stars and moons was unusually bright, and there was an earthly glow as well, a strange ghostly greenish radiance that rose in irregular patches from the slopes flanking the highway. Dekkeret asked about it. "From certain plants," said the Vroon. "They shine with an inner light in the darkness. To touch such a plant is always painful and often fatal."

"How am I to know them by daylight?"

"They look like pieces of old string, weathered and worn, sprouting in bunches from clefts in the rock. Not all the plants of such a form are dangerous, but you would do well to avoid any of them."

"And any other," Barjazid put in. "In this desert the plants are well defended, sometimes in surprising ways. Each year our garden teaches us some ugly new secret."

Dekkeret nodded. He did not plan to stroll about out there, but if he did, he would make it his rule to touch nothing.

The floater was old and slow, the grade of the highway steep. Through the broiling night the car labored unhurriedly onward. There was little conversation within. The Skandar drove, with the Vroon beside her, and occasionally Serifain Reinaulion made some comment on the condition of the road; in the rear compartment the two Barjazids sat silently, leaving Dekkeret alone to stare with growing dismay at the infernal landscape. Under the merciless hammers of the sun the ground had a beaten, broken look. Such moisture as winter had brought this land had long ago been sucked forth, leaving gaunt, angular fissures. The surface of the ground was pockmarked where the unceasing winds had strafed it with sand particles, and the plants, low and sparsely-growing things, were of many varieties but all appeared twisted, tortured, gnarled, and knobby. To the heat Dekkeret gradually

THE DESERT OF STOLEN DREAMS

found himself growing accustomed: it was simply there, like one's skin, and after a time one came to accept it. But the deathly ugliness of all that he beheld, the dry rough spiky uncaring bleakness of everything, numbed his soul. A landscape that was hateful was a new concept to him, almost an inconceivable one. Wherever he had gone on Majipoor he had known only beauty. He thought of his home city of Normork spread along the crags of the Mount, with its winding boulevards and its wondrous stone wall and its gentle midnight rains. He thought of the giant city of Stee higher on the Mount, where once he had walked at dawn in a garden of trees no taller than his ankle, with leaves of a green hue that dazzled his eyes. He thought of High Morpin, that glimmering miracle of a city devoted wholly to pleasure, that lay almost in the shadow of the Coronal's awesome castle atop the Mount. And the rugged forested wilds of Khyntor, and the brilliant white towers of Ni-moya, and the sweet meadows of the Glayge Valley—How beautiful a world this is, Dekkeret thought, and what marvels it holds, and how terrible this place I find myself in now!

He told himself that he must alter his values and strive to discover the beauties of this desert, or else it would paralyze his spirit. Let there be beauty in utter dryness, he thought, and beauty in menacing angularity, and beauty in pockmarks, and beauty in ragged plants that shine with a pale green glow by night. Let spiky be beautiful, let bleak be beautiful, let harsh be beautiful. For what is beauty, Dekkeret asked himself, if not a learned response to things beheld? Why is a meadow intrinsically more beautiful than a pebbled desert? Beauty, they say, is in the eye of the beholder; therefore re-educate your eye, Dekkeret, lest the ugliness of this land kill you.

He tried to make himself love the desert. He pulled such words as "bleak" and "dismal" and "repellent" from his mind as though pulling fangs from a wild beast, and instructed himself to see this landscape as tender and comforting. He made himself admire the contorted strata of the exposed rock faces and the great gouges of the dry washes. He found aspects of delight in the bedraggled beaten shrubs. He discovered things to esteem in the small toothy nocturnal creatures that occasionally scuttered across the road. And as the night wore on, the desert did become less hateful to him, and then neutral, and at last he believed he actually could see some beauty in it; and by the hour before dawn he had ceased to think about it at all.

Morning came suddenly: a shaft of orange flame breaking against the mountain wall to the west, a limb of bright red fire rising over the opposite rim of the range, and then the sun, its yellow face tinged more with bronzy-green than in the northern latitudes, bursting into the sky like an untethered balloon. In this moment of apocalyptic sunrise Dekkeret was startled to find himself thinking in sharp pain of the Archregimand Golator Lasgia, wondering whether she was watching the dawn, and with whom; he savored the pain a little, and then, banishing the thought, said to Barjazid, "It was a night without phantoms. Is this desert not supposed to be haunted?"

"Beyond the pass is where the real trouble begins," the little man replied.

THE DESERT OF STOLEN DREAMS

They rode onward through the early hours of the day. Dinitak served a rough breakfast, dry bread and sour wine. Looking back, Dekkeret saw a mighty view, the land sloping off below him like a great tawny apron, all folds and cracks and wrinkles, and the city of Tolaghai barely visible as a huddled clutter at the bottom end, with the vastness of the sea to the north rolling on to the horizon. The sky was without clouds, and the blue of it was so enhanced by the terra-cotta hue of the land that it seemed almost to be a second sea above him. Already the heat was rising. By mid-morning it was all but unendurable, and still the Skandar driver moved impassively up the breast of the mountain. Dekkeret dozed occasionally, but in the cramped vehicle sleep was impossible. Were they going to drive all night and then all day too? He asked no questions. But just as weariness and discomfort were reaching intolerable levels in him, Khaymak Gran abruptly swung the floater left, down a short spur of the road, and brought it to a halt.

"Our first day's camp," Barjazid announced.

Where the spur ended, a high flange of rock reared out of the desert floor, forming an overarching shelter. In front of it, protected by shadows at this time of day, was a wide sandy area that had obviously been used many times as a campsite. At the base of the rock formation Dekkeret saw a dark spot where water mysteriously seeped from the ground, not exactly a gushing spring but useful and welcome enough to parched travelers in this terrible desert. The place was ideal. And plainly the entire first day's journey had been timed to bring them here before the worst of the heat descended.

The Skandar and young Barjazid pulled straw mats from some compartment of the floater and scattered them on the sand; the midday meal was offered, chunks of dried meat, a bit of tart fruit, and warm Skandar mead; then, without a word, the two Barjazids and the Vroon and the Skandar sprawled out on their mats and dropped instantly into sleep. Dekkeret stood alone, probing between his teeth for a bit of meat caught there. Now that he could sleep, he was not at all sleepy. He wandered the edge of the campsite, staring into the sun-blasted wastes just outside the area in shadow. Not a creature could be seen, and even the plants, poor shabby things, seemed to be trying to pull themselves into the ground. The mountains rose steeply above him to the south; the pass could not be far off. And then? And then?

He tried to sleep. Unwanted images plagued him. Golator Lasgia hovered above his mat, so close that he felt he could seize her and draw her down to him, but she bobbed away and was lost in the heat-haze. For the thousandth time he saw himself in that forest in the Khyntor Marches, pursuing his prey, aiming, suddenly trembling. He shook that off and found himself scrambling along the great wall at Normork, with cool delectable air in his lungs. But these were not dreams, only idle fantasies and fugitive memories; sleep would not come for a long time, and when it did, it was deep and dreamless and brief.

Strange sounds awakened him: humming, singing, musical instruments in the distance, the faint but

THE DESERT OF STOLEN DREAMS

distinct noises of a caravan of many travelers. He thought he heard the tinkle of bells, the booming of drums. For a time he lay still, listening, trying to understand. Then he sat up, blinked, looked around. Twilight had come. He had slept away the hottest part of the day, and the shadows now encroached from the other side. His four companions were up and packing the mats. Dekkeret cocked an ear, seeking the source of the sounds. But they seemed to come from everywhere, or from nowhere. He remembered Golator Lasgia's tale of the ghosts of the desert that sing by day, confusing travelers, leading them from the true path with their clatter and their music.

To Barjazid he said, "What are those sounds?"

"Sounds?"

"You don't hear them? Voices, bells, footfalls, the humming of many travelers?"

Barjazid looked amused. "You mean the desert-songs."

"Ghost-songs?"

"They could be that. Or merely the sounds of wayfarers coming down the mountain, rattling chains, striking gongs. Which is more probable?"

"Neither is probable," said Dekkeret gloomily. "There are no ghosts in the world I inhabit. But there are no wayfarers on this road except ourselves."

"Are you sure, Initiate?"

"That there are no wayfarers, or no ghosts?"

"Either."

Dinitak Barjazid, who had been standing to one side taking in this interchange, approached Dekkeret and said, "Are you frightened?"

"The unknown is always disturbing. But at this point I feel more curiosity than fear."

"I will gratify your curiosity, then. As the heat of the day diminishes, the rocky cliffs and the sands give up their warmth, and in cooling they contract and release sounds. Those are the drums and bells you hear. There are no ghosts in this place," the boy said.

The elder Barjazid made a brusque gesture. Serenely the boy moved away.

"You didn't want him to tell me that, did you?" Dekkeret asked. "You prefer me to think that there are ghosts all about me."

Smiling, Barjazid said, "It makes no difference to me. Believe whichever explanation you find more cheering. You will meet a sufficiency of ghosts, I assure you, on the far side of the pass."

VII

LL STARDAY EVENING they climbed the winding road up the face of the mountain, and near midnight came to Khulag Pass. Here the air was cooler, for they were thousands of feet above sea level and warring winds brought some relief from the swelter. The pass was a broad notch in the mountain wall, surprisingly deep; it was early Sunday morning before they completed its traversal and began their descent into the greater desert of the interior.

Dekkeret was stunned by what lay before him. By bright moonlight he beheld a scene of unparalleled bleakness, that made the lands on the cityward side of the pass look like gardens. That other desert was a rocky one, but this was sandy, an ocean of dunes broken here and there by open patches of hard pebble-strewn ground. There was scarcely any vegetation, none at all in the duned places and the merest of sorry scraggles elsewhere. And the heat! Upward out of the dark bowl ahead there came currents of stupefying hot blasts, air that seemed stripped of all nourishment, air that had been baked to death. It astounded him that somewhere in that furnace there could be grazing lands. He tried to remember the map in the Archregimand's office: the cattle country was a belt that flanked the continent's innermost zone of desert, but here below Khulag Pass an arm of the central wastes had somehow encroached—that was it. On the far side of this band of formidable sterility lay a green zone of grass and browsing beasts, or so he prayed.

Through the early morning hours they headed down the inner face of the mountains and onto the great central plateau. By first light Dekkeret noticed an odd feature far downslope, an oval patch of inky darkness sharply outlined against the buff breast of the desert, and as they drew nearer he saw that it was an oasis of sorts, the dark patch resolving itself into a grove of slender long-limbed trees with tiny violet-flushed leaves. This place was the second day's campsite. Tracks in the sand showed where other parties had camped; there was scattered debris under the trees; in a clearing at the heart of the grove were half a dozen crude shelters made of heaped-up rocks topped with old dried boughs. Just beyond, a brackish stream wound between the trees and terminated in a small stagnant pool, green with algae. And a little way beyond that was a second pool, apparently fed by a stream that ran wholly underground, the waters of which were pure. Between the two pools Dekkeret saw a curious construction, seven round-topped stone columns as high as his waist, arranged in a double arc. He inspected them.

"Shapeshifter work," Barjazid told him.

"A Metamorph altar?"

"So we think. We know the Shapeshifters often visit this oasis. We find little Piurivar souvenirs here—

prayer sticks, bits of feathers, small clever wickerwork cups."

Dekkeret stared about uneasily at the trees as if he expected them to transform themselves momentarily into a party of savage aborigines. He had had little contact with the native race of Majipoor, those defeated and displaced indigenes of the forests, and what he knew of them was mainly rumor and fantasy, born of fear, ignorance, and guilt. They once had had great cities, that much was certain—Alhanroel was strewn with the ruins of them, and in school Dekkeret had seen views of the most famous of all, vast stone Velalisier not far from the Labyrinth of the Pontifex; but those cities had died thousands of years ago, and with the coming of the human and other races to Majipoor the native Piurivars had been forced back into the darker places of the planet, mainly a great wooded reservation in Zimroel somewhere southeast of Khyntor. To his knowledge Dekkeret had seen actual Metamorphs only two or three times, frail greenish folk with strange blank-featured faces, but of course they slid from one form to another in mimicry of a marvelously easy kind. For all he knew this little Vroon here was a secret Shapeshifter, or Barjazid himself.

He said, "How can Shapeshifters or anyone else survive in this desert?"

"They're resourceful people. They adapt."

"Are there many of them here?"

"Who can know? I've encountered a few scattered bands, fifty, seventy-five all told. Probably there are others. Or perhaps I keep meeting the same ones over and over again in different guises, eh?"

"A strange people," Dekkeret said, rubbing his hand idly over the smooth stone dome atop the nearest of the altar-columns. With astonishing speed Barjazid grasped Dekkeret's wrist and pulled it back.

"Don't touch those!"

"Why not?" said Dekkeret, amazed.

"Those stones are holy."

"To you?"

"To those who erected them," said Barjazid dourly. "We respect them. We honor the magic that may be in them. And in this land one never casually invites the vengeance of one's neighbors."

Dekkeret stared in astonishment at the little man, at the columns, at the two pools, the graceful sharp-leaved trees that surrounded them. Even in the heat he shivered. He looked out, beyond the borders of the little oasis, to the swaybacked dunes all around, to the dusty ribbon of road that disappeared southward into the land of mysteries. The sun was climbing quickly now and its warmth was like a terrible flail pounding the sky, the land, the few vulnerable travelers wandering in this awful place. He glanced back, to the mountains he had just passed through, a huge and ominous wall cutting him off from what passed for civilization on this torrid continent. He felt frighteningly alone here, weak, lost.

Dinitak Barjazid appeared, tottering under a great load of flasks that he dropped almost at Dekkeret's feet. Dekkeret helped the boy fill them from the pure pool, a task that took an unexpectedly long while. He sampled the water himself: cool, clear, with a strange metallic taste, not displeasing, that Dinitak said came from dis-

THE DESERT OF STOLEN DREAMS

solved minerals. It took a dozen trips to carry all the flasks to the floater. There would be no more sources of fresh water, Dinitak explained, for several days.

They lunched on the usual rough provisions and afterward, as the heat rose toward its overwhelming midday peak, they settled on the straw mats to sleep. This was the third day that Dekkeret had slept by day and by now his body was growing attuned to the change; he closed his eyes, commended his soul to the beloved Lady of the Isle, Lord Prestimion's holy mother, and tumbled almost instantly into heavy slumber.

This time dreams came.

He had not dreamed properly for more days than he cared to remember. To Dekkeret as to all other folk of Majipoor dreams were a central part of existence, nightly providing comfort, reassurance, instruction, clarification, guidance and reprimands, and much else. From childhood one was trained to make one's mind receptive to the messengers of sleep, to observe and record one's dreams, to carry them with one through the night and into the waking hours beyond. And always there was the benevolent omnipresent figure of the Lady of the Isle of Sleep hovering over one, helping one explore the workings of one's spirit and through her sendings offering direct communication to each of the billions of souls that dwelled on vast Majipoor.

Dekkeret now saw himself walking on a mountain ridge that he perceived to be the crest of the range they had lately crossed. He was by himself and the sun was impossibly great, filling half the sky; yet the heat was not troublesome. So steep was the slope that he could look straight down over the edge, down and down and down for what seemed hundreds of miles, and he beheld a roaring smoking cauldron beneath him, a surging volcanic crater in which red magma bubbled and churned. That immense vortex of subterranean power did not frighten him; indeed it exerted a strange pull, a blatant appeal, so that he yearned to plunge himself into it, to dive to its depths and swim in its molten heart. He began to descend, running and skipping, often leaving the ground and floating, drifting, flying down the immense hillside, and as he drew nearer he thought he saw faces in the throbbing lava, Lord Prestimion, and the Pontifex, and Barjazid's face, and Golator Lasgia's—and were those Metamorphs, those strange sly half-visible images near the periphery? The core of the volcano was a stew of potent figures. Dekkeret ran toward them in love, thinking, Take me into you, here I am, here I come; and when he perceived, behind all the others, a great white disk that he understood to be the loving countenance of the Lady of the Isle, a deep and powerful bliss invaded his soul, for he knew this now to be a sending, and it was many months since last the kind Lady had touched his sleeping mind.

Sleeping but aware, watching the Dekkeret within the dream, he awaited the consummation, the joining of dream-Dekkeret to dream-Lady, the immolation in the volcano that would bring some revelation of truth, some instant of knowledge leading to joy. But then a strangeness crossed the dream like some spreading veil. The colors faded; the faces dimmed; he continued to run down the side of the mountain wall, but now he

THE DESERT OF STOLEN DREAMS

stumbled often, he tripped and sprawled, he abraded his hands and knees against hot desert rocks, and he was losing the path entirely, moving sideways instead of downward, unable to progress. He had been on the verge of a moment of delight, and somehow it was out of reach now and he felt only distress, uneasiness, shock. The ecstasy that seemed to be the promise of the dream was draining from it. The brilliant colors yielded to an all-encompassing gray, and all motion ceased: he stood frozen on the mountain face, staring rigidly down at a dead crater, and the sight of it made him tremble and pull his knees to his chest, and he lay there sobbing until he woke.

He blinked and sat up. His head pounded and his eyes felt raw, and there was a dismal tension in his chest and shoulders. This was not what dreams, even the most terrifying of dreams, were supposed to provide: such a gritty residue of malaise, confusion, fear. It was early afternoon and the blinding sun hung high above the treetops. Nearby him lay Khaymak Gran and the Vroon, Serifain Reinaulion; a bit farther away was Dinitak Barjazid. They seemed sound asleep. The elder Barjazid was nowhere in view. Dekkeret rolled over and pressed his cheeks into the warm sand beside his mat and attempted to let the tension ease from him. Something had gone wrong in his sleep, he knew; some dark force had meddled in his dream, had stolen the virtue from it and given him pain in exchange. So this was what they meant by the haunting of the desert? This was dream-stealing? He drew himself together in a knotted ball. He felt soiled, used, invaded. He wondered if it would be like this every sleep-period now, as they penetrated deeper into this awful desert; he wondered whether it might get even worse.

After a time Dekkeret returned to sleep. More dreams came, stray blurred scraps without rhythm or design. He ignored them. When he woke, the day was ending and the desert-sounds, the ghost-sounds, were nibbling at his ears, tinklings and murmurings and far-off laughter. He felt more weary than if he had not slept at all.

VIII

HE OTHERS showed no sign of having been disturbed as they slept. They greeted Dekkeret upon rising in their usual manners—the huge taciturn Skandar woman not at all, the little Vroon with amiable buzzing chirps and much coiling and interlacing of tentacles, the two Barjazids with curt nods—and if they were aware that one member of their party had been visited with torments in his dreams, they said nothing of it. After breakfast the elder Barjazid held a brief conference with Serifain Reinaulion concerning the roads they were to travel that night, and then they were off into the moonlit darkness once again.

I will pretend that nothing out of the ordinary happened, Dekkeret resolved. I will not let them know that I am vulnerable to these phantoms.

But it was a short-lived resolution. As the floater was passing through a region of dry lakebeds out of which odd gray-green stony humps projected by the thousands, Barjazid turned to him suddenly and said, breaking a long silence, "Did you dream well?"

Dekkeret knew he could not conceal his fatigue. "I have had better rest," he muttered.

Barjazid's glossy eyes were fixed inexorably on his. "My son says you moaned in your sleep, that you rolled over many times and clutched your knees. Did you feel the touch of the dream-stealers, Initiate?"

"I felt the presence of a troubling power in my dreams. Whether this was the touch of the dream-stealers I have no way of knowing."

"Will you describe the sensations?"

"Are you a dream-speaker then, Barjazid?" Dekkeret snapped in sudden anger. "Why should I let you probe and poke in my mind? My dreams are my own!"

"Peace, peace, good knight. I meant no intrusion."

"Let me be, then."

"Your safety is my responsibility. If the demons of this wasteland have begun to reach your spirit, it is in your own interest to inform me."

"Demons, are they?"

"Demons, ghosts, phantoms, disaffected Shapeshifters, whatever they are," Barjazid said impatiently. "The beings that prey on sleeping travelers. Did they come to you or did they not?"

"My dreams were not pleasing."

"I ask you to tell me in what way."

Dekkeret let his breath out slowly. "I felt I was having a sending from the Lady, a dream of peace and joy. And gradually it changed its nature, do you see? It darkened and became chaotic, and all the joy was taken from it, and I ended the dream worse than when I entered it."

Nodding earnestly, Barjazid said, "Yes, yes, those are the symptoms. A touch on the mind, an invasion of the dream, a disturbing overlay, a taking of energy."

"A kind of vampirism?" Dekkeret suggested. "Creatures that lie in wait in this wasteland and tap the life-

THE DESERT OF STOLEN DREAMS

force from unwary travelers?"

Barjazid smiled. "You insist on speculations. I make no hypotheses of any kind, Initiate."

"Have you felt their touch in your own sleep?"

The small man stared at Dekkeret strangely. "No. No, never."

"Never? Are you immune?"

"Seemingly so."

"And your boy?"

"It has befallen him several times. It happens to him only rarely out here, one time out of fifty, perhaps. But the immunity is not hereditary, it appears."

"And the Skandar? And the Vroon?"

"They too have been touched," said Barjazid. "On infrequent occasions. They find it bothersome but not intolerable."

"Yet others have died from the dream-stealers' touch."

"More hypothesis," said Barjazid. "Most travelers passing this way in recent years have reported experiencing strange dreams. Some of them have lost their way and have failed to return. How can we know whether there is a connection between the disturbing dreams and the losing of the way?"

"You are a very cautious man," Dekkeret said. "You leap to no conclusions."

"And I have survived to a fair old age, while many who were more rash have returned to the Source."

"Is mere survival the highest achievement you think one can attain?"

Barjazid laughed. "Spoken like a true knight of the Castle! No, Initiate, I think there's more to living than mere avoidance of death. But survival helps, eh, Initiate? Survival's a good basic requirement for those who go on to do high deeds. The dead don't achieve a thing."

Dekkeret did not care to pursue that theme. The code of values of a knight-initiate and of such a one as Barjazid were hardly comparable; and, besides, there was something wily and mercurial about Barjazid's style of argument that made Dekkeret feel slow and stolid and hulking, and he disliked exposing himself to that feeling. He was silent a moment. Then he said, "Do the dreams get worse as one gets deeper into the desert?"

"So I am given to understand," said Barjazid.

Yet as the night waned and the time for making camp arrived, Dekkeret found himself ready and even eager to contend once more with the phantoms of sleep. They had camped this day far out on the bowl of the desert, in a low-lying area where much of the sand had been swept aside by scouring winds, and the underlying rock shield showed through. The dry air had a weird crackle to it, a kind of wind-borne buzz, as if the force of the sun were stripping the particles of matter bare in this place. It was only an hour before midday by the time they were ready for sleep. Dekkeret settled calmly on his mat of straw and, without fear, offered his soul on the verge of slumber to whatever might come. In his order of knighthood he had been trained in the customary notions of courage, naturally, and was expected to meet challenges without fear, but he had been little tested thus far. On placid Majipoor one must work hard to find such challenges, going into the untamed parts of the world, for in the settled regions life is orderly and courteous; therefore Dekkeret had gone abroad, but he had not done well by his first major trial, in the forests of the Khyntor Marches. Here he had another chance. These foul dreams held forth to him, in a way, the promise of redemption.

He gave himself up to sleep.

And quickly dreamed. He was back in Tolaghai, but a Tolaghai curiously transformed, a city of smooth-faced alabaster villas and dense green gardens, though the heat was still of tropical intensity. He wandered up one boulevard and down the next, admiring the elegance of the architecture and the splendor of the shrubbery. His clothing was the traditional green-and-gold of the Coronal's entourage, and as he encountered the citizens of Tolaghai making their twilight promenades he bowed gracefully to them, and exchanged with them the starburst finger-symbol that acknowledged the Coronal's authority. To him now came the slender figure of the lovely Archregimand Golator Lasgia. She smiled, she took him by the hand, she led him to a place of cascading fountains where cool spray drifted through the air, and there they put their clothing aside and bathed, and rose naked from the sweet-scented pool, and strolled, feet barely touching the ground, into a garden of plants with arching stems and great glistening many-lobed leaves. Without words she encouraged him onward, along shadowy avenues bordered by rows of close-planted trees. Golator Lasgia moved just ahead of him, an elusive and tantalizing figure, floating only inches out of his reach and then gradually widening the distance to feet and yards. At first it seemed hardly a difficult task to overtake her, but he made no headway at it, and had to move faster and faster to keep within sight of her. Her rich olive-hued skin gleamed by early moonlight, and she glanced back often, smiling brilliantly, tossing her head to urge him to keep up. But he could not. She was nearly an entire length of the garden ahead of him now. With growing desperation he impelled himself toward her, but she was dwindling, disappearing, so far ahead of him now that he could barely see the play of muscles beneath her glowing bare skin, and as he rushed from one pathway of the garden to the next he became aware of an increase in the temperature, a sudden and steady change in the air, for somehow the sun was rising here in the night and its full force was striking his shoulders. The trees were wilting and drooping. Leaves were falling. He struggled to remain upright. Golator Lasgia was only a dot on the horizon now, still beckoning to him, still smiling, still tossing her head, but she grew smaller and smaller, and the sun was still climbing, growing stronger, searing, incinerating, withering everything within its reach. Now the garden was a place of gaunt bare branches and rough cracked arid soil. A dreadful thirst had come over him, but there was no water here, and when he saw figures lurking behind the blistered and blackened trees—Metamorphs, they were, subtle tricky creatures that would not hold their shapes still but flickered and flowed in a maddening way—he called out to them for something to drink, and was given only light tinkling laughter to ease his dryness. He staggered on. The fierce pulsing light in the heavens was beginning to roast him; he felt his skin hardening, crackling, crisping, splitting. Another moment of this and he would be charred. What had become of Golator Lasgia? Where were the smiling, bowing, starburst-making townspeople? He saw no garden now. He was in the desert, lurching and stumbling through a torrid baking wasteland where even shadows burned. Now real terror rose in him, for even as he dreamed he felt the pain of the heat, and the part of his soul that was observing all this grew alarmed, thinking that the power of the dream might well be so great as to reach up to injure his physical self. There were tales of such things, people who had perished in their sleep of dreams that had overwhelming force. Although it went against his training to terminate a dream prematurely, although he knew he must ordinarily see even the worst of horrors through to its ultimate revelation, Dekkeret considered awakening himself for safety's sake, and nearly did; but then he saw that as a species of cowardice and vowed to remain in the dream even if it cost him his life. He was down on his knees now, groveling in the fiery sands, staring with strange clarity at mysterious tiny golden-bodied insects that were marching in single file across the rims of the dunes toward him: ants, they were, with ugly swollen jaws, and each in turn clambered up his body and took a tiny nip, the merest bite, and clung and held on, so that within moments thousands of the minute creatures were covering his skin. He brushed at them but could not dislodge them. Their pincers held and their heads came loose from their bodies: the sand about him was black now with headless ants, but they spread over his skin like a cloak, and he brushed and brushed with greater vigor while still more ants mounted him and dug their jaws in. He grew weary of brushing at them. It was actually cooler in this cloak of ants, he thought. They shielded him from the worst force of the sun, although they too stung and burned him, but not as painfully as did the sun's rays. Would the dream never end? He attempted to take control of it himself, to turn the stream of onrushing ants into a rivulet of cool pure water, but that did not work, and he let himself slip back into the nightmare and went crawling wearily onward over the sands.

And gradually Dekkeret became aware that he was no longer dreaming.

There was no boundary between sleep and wakefulness that he could detect, except that eventually he realized that his eyes were open and that his two centers of consciousness, the dreamer who observed and the dream-Dekkeret who suffered, had merged into one. But he was still in the desert, under the terrible midday sun. He was naked. His skin felt raw and blistered. And there were ants crawling on him, up his legs as far as his knees, minute pale ants that indeed were nipping their tiny pincers into his flesh. Bewildered, he wondered if he had tumbled into some layer of dream beneath dream, but no, so far as he could tell this was the waking world, this was the authentic desert and he was out in the midst of it. He stood up, brushing the ants away—and as in the dream they gripped him even at the cost of their heads—and looked about for the campsite.

He could not see it. In his sleep he had wandered out onto the bare scorching anvil of the open desert and he was lost. Let this be a dream still, he thought fiercely, and let me awaken from it in the shade of Barjazid's floater. But there was no awakening. Dekkeret understood now how lives were lost in the Desert of Stolen Dreams.

"Barjazid?" he called. "*Barjazid!*"

IX

ECHOES CAME BACK to him from the distant hills. He called again, two, three times, and listened to the reverberations of his own voice, but heard no reply. How long could he survive out here? An hour? Two? He had no water, no shelter, not even a scrap of clothing. His head was bare to the sun's great blazing eye. It was the hottest part of the day. The landscape looked the same in all directions, flat, a shallow bowl swept by hot winds. He searched for his own footprints, but the trail gave out within yards, for the ground was hard and rocky here and he had left no imprint. The camp might lie anywhere about, hidden from him by the slightest of rises in the terrain. He called out again for help and again heard only echoes. Perhaps if he could find a dune he would bury himself to his neck, and wait out the heat that way, and by darkness he might find the camp by its campfire; but he saw no dunes. If there were a high place here that would give him a sweeping view, he would mount it and search the horizon for the camp. But he saw no hillocks. What would Lord Stiamot do in such a situation, he wondered, or Lord Thimin, or one of the other great warriors of the past? What is Dekkeret going to do? This was a foolish way to die, he thought, a useless, nasty, ugly death. He turned and

THE DESERT OF STOLEN DREAMS

turned and turned again, scanning every way. No clues; no point in walking at all, not knowing where he was going. He shrugged and crouched in a place where there were no ants. There was no dazzlingly clever ploy that he could use to save himself. There was no inner resource that would bring him, against all the odds, to safety. He had lost himself in his sleep, and he would die just as Golator Lasgia had said he would, and that was all there was to it. Only one thing remained to him, and that was strength of character: he would die quietly and calmly, without tears or anger, without raging against the forces of fate. Perhaps it would take an hour. Perhaps less. The important thing was to die honorably, for when death is inevitable there's no sense making a botch of it.

He waited for it to come.

What came instead—ten minutes later, half an hour, an hour, he had no way of knowing—was Serifain Reinaulion. The Vroon appeared like a mirage out of the east, trudging slowly toward Dekkeret struggling under the weight of two flasks of water, and when he was within a hundred yards or so he waved two of his tentacles and called, "Are you alive?"

"More or less. Are you real?"

"Real enough. And we've been searching for you half the afternoon." In a flurry of rubbery limbs the small creature pushed one of the flasks upward into Dekkeret's hands. "Here. Sip it. Don't gulp. *Don't gulp.* You're so dehydrated you'll drown if you're too greedy."

Dekkeret fought the impulse to drain the flask in one long pull. The Vroon was right: sip, sip, be moderate, or harm will come. He let the water trickle into his mouth, swished it around, soaked his swollen tongue in it, finally let it down his throat. *Ah.* Another cautious sip. Another, then a fair swallow. He grew a little dizzy. Serifain Reinaulion beckoned for the flask. Dekkeret shook him off, drank again, rubbed a little of the water against his cheeks and lips.

"How far are we from the camp?" he asked finally.

"Ten minutes. Are you strong enough to walk, or shall I go back for the others?"

"I can walk."

"Let's get started, then."

Dekkeret nodded. "One more little sip—"

"Carry the flask. Drink whenever you like. If you get weak, tell me and we'll rest. Remember, I can't carry you."

The Vroon headed off slowly toward a low sandy ridge perhaps five hundred yards to the east. Feeling wobbly and lightheaded, Dekkeret followed, and was surprised to see the ground trending upward; the ridge was not all that low, he realized, but some trick of the glare had made him think otherwise. In fact it rose to two or three times his own height, high enough to conceal two lesser ridges on the far side. The floater was parked in the shadow of the farther one.

Barjazid was the only person at the camp. He glanced up at Dekkeret with what looked like contempt or annoyance in his eyes and said, "Went for a stroll, did you? At noontime?"

"Sleepwalking. The dream-stealers had me. It was like being under a spell." Dekkeret was shivering as the sunburn began to disrupt his body's heat-shedding systems. He dropped down alongside the floater and huddled under a light robe. "When I woke I couldn't see camp. I was sure that I would die."

"Half an hour more and you would have. You must be two-thirds fried as it is. Lucky for you my boy woke up and saw that you had disappeared."

Dekkeret pulled the robe tighter around him. "Is that how they die out here? By sleepwalking at midday?"

"One of the ways, yes."

"I owe you my life."

"You've owed me your life since we crossed Khulag Pass. Going on your own you'd have been dead fifty times already. But thank the Vroon, if you have to thank anyone. He did the real work of finding you."

Dekkeret nodded. "Where's your son? And Khaymak Gran? Out looking for me also?"

"On their way back," said Barjazid. And indeed the Skandar and the boy appeared only moments later. Without a glance at him the Skandar flung herself down on her sleeping-mat; Dinitak Barjazid grinned slyly at Dekkeret and said, "Had a pleasant walk?"

"Not very. I regret the inconvenience I caused you."

"As do we."

"Perhaps I should sleep tied down from now on."

"Or with a heavy weight sitting on your chest," Dinitak suggested. He yawned. "Try to stay put until sundown, at least. Will you?"

"So I intend," said Dekkeret.

But it was impossible for him to fall asleep. His skin itched in a thousand places from the bites of the insects, and the sunburn, despite a cooling ointment that Serifain Reinaulion gave him, made him miserable. There was a dry, dusty feeling in his throat that no amount of water seemed to cure, and his eyes throbbed painfully. As though probing an irritating sore he ran through his memories of his desert ordeal again and again—the dream, the heat, the ants, the thirst, the awareness of imminent death. Rigorously he searched for moments of cowardice and found none. Dismay, yes, and anger, and discomfort, but he had no recollection of panic or fear. Good. Good. The worst part of the experience, he decided, had not been the heat and thirst and peril but the dream, the dark and disturbing dream, the dream that had once again begun in joy and midway had undergone a somber metamorphosis. To be denied the solace of healthy dreams is a kind of death-in-life, he thought, far worse than perishing in a desert, for dying occupies only a single moment but dreaming affects all of one's time to come. And what knowledge was it that these bleak Suvraelu dreams were imparting? Dekkeret knew that when dreams came from the Lady they must be studied intently, if necessary with the aid of one who practices the art of dream-speaking, for they contain information vital to the proper conduct of one's life; but these dreams were hardly of the Lady, seeming rather to emanate from some other dark Power, some sinister and oppressive force more adept at taking than giving. Shapeshifters? It could be. What if some tribe of them had, through deceit, obtained one of the devices by which the Lady of the Isle is able to reach the minds of her flock, and lurked here in the hot heartland of Suvrael preying on unwary travelers, stealing from their souls, draining their vitality, imposing an unknown and unfathomable revenge one by one upon those who had stolen their world? Dekkeret saw now how important it was for him to survive this journey. He had to bring to the government word of a danger in this land far more serious than a mere trade imbalance.

As the afternoon shadows lengthened he found himself at last slipping back into sleep. He fought it, fearing the touch of the invisible intruders on his soul once again. Desperately he held his eyes open, staring across the darkening wasteland and listening to the eerie hum and buzz of the desert-sounds; but it was impossible to fend off the exhaustion longer. He drifted into a light, uneasy slumber, broken from time to time by dreams that he sensed came neither from the Lady nor from any other external force, but merely floated randomly through the strata of his weary mind, bits of patternless incident and stray incomprehensible images. And then someone was shaking him awake—the Vroon, he realized. Dekkeret's mind was foggy and slow. He felt numbed. His lips were cracked, his back was sore. Night had fallen, and his companions were already at work closing down their camp. Serifain Reinaulion offered Dekkeret a cup of some sweet thick blue-green juice, and he drank it in a single draught.

"Come," the Vroon said. "Time to be going onward."

X

OW THE DESERT CHANGED again and the landscape grew violent and rough. Evidently there had been great earthquakes here, and more than one, for the land lay fractured and upheaved, with mighty blocks of the desert floor piled at unlikely angles against others, and huge sprawls of talus at the feet of the low shattered cliffs. Through this chaotic zone of turbulence and disruption there was only a single passable route—the wide, gently curving bed of a long-extinct river whose sandy floor swerved in long easy bends between the cracked and sundered rock-heaps. The large moon was full and there was almost a daylight brilliance to the grotesque scene. After some hours of passing through a terrain so much the same from one mile to the next that it seemed almost as though the floater were not moving at all, Dekkeret turned to Barjazid and said, "And how long will it be before we reach Ghyzyn Kor?"

"This valley marks the boundary between desert and grazing-lands." Barjazid pointed toward the southwest, where the riverbed vanished between two towering craggy peaks that rose like daggers from the desert floor. "Beyond that place—Munnerak Notch—the

THE DESERT OF STOLEN DREAMS

climate is altogether different. On the far side of the mountain wall sea-fogs enter by night from the west, and the land is green and fit for grazing. We will camp halfway to the Notch tomorrow, and pass through it the day after. By Seaday at the latest you'll be at your lodgings in Ghyzyn Kor."

"And you?" Dekkeret asked.

"My son and I have business elsewhere in the area. We'll return to Ghyzyn Kor for you after—three days? Five?"

"Five should be sufficient."

"Yes. And then the return journey."

"By the same route?"

"There is no other," said Barjazid. "They explained to you in Tolaghai, did they not, that access to the rangelands was cut off, except by way of this desert? But why should you fear this route? The dreams aren't so awful, are they? And so long as you do no more roaming in your sleep, you'll not be in any danger here."

It sounded simple enough. Indeed he felt sure he could survive the trip; but yesterday's dream had been sufficient torment, and he looked without cheer upon what might yet come. When they made camp the next morning Dekkeret found himself again uneasy about entrusting himself to sleep at all. For the first hour of the rest-period he kept himself awake, listening to the metallic clangor of the bare tumbled rocks as they stretched and quivered in the midday heat, until at last sleep came up over his mind like a dense black cloud and took him unawares.

And in time a dream possessed him, and it was, he knew at its outset, going to be the most terrible of all.

Pain came first—an ache, a twinge, a pang, then without warning a racking explosion of dazzling light against the walls of his skull, making him grunt and clutch his head. The agonizing spasm passed swiftly, though, and he felt the soft sleek presence of Golator Lasgia about him, soothing him, cradling him against her breasts. She rocked him and murmured to him and eased him until he opened his eyes and sat up and looked around, and saw that he was out of the desert, free of Suvrael itself. He and Golator Lasgia were in some cool forest glade where giant trees with perfectly straight yellow-barked trunks rose to incomprehensible heights, and a swiftly flowing stream, studded with rocky outcroppings, tumbled and roared wildly past almost at their feet. Beyond the stream the land dropped sharply away, revealing a distant valley, and, on the far side of it, a great gray saw-toothed snow-capped mountain which Dekkeret recognized instantly as one of the nine vast peaks of the Khyntor Marches.

"No," he said. "This is not where I want to be."

Golator Lasgia laughed, and the pretty tinkling sound of it was somewhat sinister in his ears, like the delicate sounds the desert made at twilight. "But this is a dream, good friend! You must take what comes, in dreams!"

"I will direct my dream. I have no wish to return to the Khyntor Marches. Look: the scene changes. We are on the Zimr, approaching the river's great bend. See? See? The city of Ni-moya sparkling there before us?"

Indeed he saw the huge city, white against the green backdrop of forested hills. But Golator Lasgia shook her head.

"There is no city here, my love. There is only the northern forest. Feel the wind? Listen to the song of the stream. Here—kneel, scoop up the fallen needles on the ground. Ni-moya is far away, and we are here to hunt."

"I beg you, let us be in Ni-moya."

"Another time," said Golator Lasgia.

He could not prevail. The magical towers of Ni-moya wavered and grew transparent and were gone, and there remained only the yellow-boled trees, the chilly breezes, the sounds of the forest. Dekkeret trembled. He was the prisoner of this dream and there was no escape.

And now five hunters in rough black haigus-hide robes appeared and made perfunctory gestures of deference and held forth weapons to him, the blunt dull tube of an energy-thrower and a short sparkling poniard and a blade of a longer kind with a hooked tip. He shook his head, and one of the hunters came close and grinned mockingly at him, a gap-toothed grin out of a wide mouth stinking from dried fish. Dekkeret recognized her face, and looked away in shame, for she was the hunter who had died on that other day in the Khyntor Marches a thousand years ago. If only she were not here now, he thought, the dream might be bearable. But this was diabolical torture, to force him to live through all this once again.

Golator Lasgia said, "Take the weapons from her. The steetmoy are running and we must be after them."

"I have no wish to—"

"What folly, to think that dreams respect wishes! The dream *is* your wish. Take the weapons."

Dekkeret understood. With chilled fingers he accepted the blades and the energy-thrower and stowed them in the proper places on his belt. The hunters smiled and grunted things at him in the thick harsh dialect of the north. Then they began to run along the bank of the stream, moving in easy loping bounds, touching the ground no more than one stride out of five; and willy-nilly Dekkeret ran with them, clumsily at first, then with much the same floating grace. Golator Lasgia, by his side, kept pace easily, her dark hair fluttering about her face, her eyes bright with excitement. They turned left, into the heart of the forest, and fanned out in a crescent formation that widened and curved inward to confront the prey.

The prey! Dekkeret could see three white-furred steetmoy gleaming like lanterns deep in the forest. The beasts prowled uneasily, growling, aware of intruders but still unwilling to abandon their territory—big crea-tures, possibly the most dangerous wild animals on Majipoor, quick and powerful and cunning, the terrors of the northlands. Dekkeret drew his poniard. Killing steetmoy with energy-throwers was no sport, and might damage too much of their valuable fur besides: one was supposed to get to close range and kill them with one's blade, preferably the poniard, if necessary the hooked machete.

The hunters looked to him. Pick one, they were saying, choose your quarry. Dekkeret nodded. The middle one, he indicated. They were smiling coldly. What did they know that they were not telling him? It had been like this that other time, too, the barely concealed scorn of the mountain folk for the pampered lordlings who were seeking deadly amusements in their forests; and that outing had ended badly. Dekkeret hefted his poniard. The dream-steetmoy that moved nervously beyond those trees were implausibly enormous, great heavy-haunched immensities that clearly could not be slain by one man alone, wielding only hand-weapons, but here there was no turning back, for he knew himself to be bound upon whatever destiny the dream offered him. Now with hunting-horns and hand-clapping the hired hunters commenced to stampede the prey; the steetmoy, angered and baffled by the sudden blaring strident sounds, rose high, whirled, raked trees with their claws, swung around, and more in disgust than fear began to run.

The chase was on.

Dekkeret knew that the hunters were separating the animals, driving the two rejected ones away to allow him a clear chance at the one he had chosen. But he looked neither to the right nor the left. Accompanied by Golator Lasgia and one of the hunters, he rushed forward, giving pursuit as the steetmoy in the center went rumbling and crashing through the forest. This was the worst part, for although humans were faster, steetmoy were better able to break through barriers of underbrush, and he might well lose his quarry altogether in the confusions of the run. The forest here was fairly open; but the steetmoy was heading for cover, and soon Dekkeret found himself struggling past saplings and vines and low brush, barely able to keep the retreating white phantom in view. With singleminded intensity he ran and hacked with the machete and clambered through thickets. It was all so terribly familiar, so much of an old story, especially when he realized that the steetmoy was doubling back, was looping through the trampled part of the forest as if planning a counterattack—

The moment would soon be at hand, the dreaming Dekkeret knew, when the maddened animal would blunder upon the gap-toothed hunter, would seize the mountain woman and hurl her against a tree, and Dekkeret, unwilling or unable to halt, would go plunging onward, continuing the chase, leaving the woman where she lay, so that when the squat thick-snouted scavenging beast emerged from its hole and began to rip her belly apart there would be no one to defend her, and only later, when things were more quiet and there was time to go back for the injured hunter, would he begin to regret the callous uncaring focus of concentration that had allowed him to ignore his fallen companion for the sake of keeping sight of his prey. And afterward the shame, the guilt, the unending self-accusations—yes, he would go through all that again as he lay here asleep in the stifling heat of the Suvraelu desert, would he not?

No.

No, it was not that simple at all, for the language of dreams is complex, and in the thick mists that suddenly enfolded the forest Dekkeret saw the steetmoy swing

THE DESERT OF STOLEN DREAMS

around and lash the gap-toothed woman and knock her flat, but the woman rose and spat out a few bloody teeth and laughed, and the chase continued, or rather it twisted back on itself to the same point, the steetmoy bursting forth unexpectedly from the darkest part of the woods and striking at Dekkeret himself, knocking his poniard and his machete from his hands, rearing high overhead for the death-blow, but not delivering it, for the image changed and it ws Golator Lasgia who lay beneath the plunging claws while Dekkeret wandered aimlessly nearby, unable to move in any useful direction, and then it was the huntswoman who was the victim once more, and Dekkeret again, and suddenly and improbably old pinch-faced Barjazid, and then Golator Lasgia. As Dekkeret watched, a voice at his elbow said, "What does it matter? We each owe the Divine a death. Perhaps it was more important for you then to follow your prey." Dekkeret stared. The voice was the voice of the gap-toothed hunter. The sound of it left him dazed and shaking. The dream was becoming bewildering. He struggled to penetrate its mysteries.

Now he saw Barjazid standing at his side in the dark cool forest glade. The steetmoy once more was savaging the mountain woman.

"Is this the way it truly was?" Barjazid asked.
"I suppose so. I didn't see it."
"What did you do?"
"Kept on going. I didn't want to lose the animal."
"You killed it?"
"Yes."
"And then?"

"Came back. And found her. Like that—"

Dekkeret pointed. The snuffling scavenger was astride the woman. Golator Lasgia stood nearby, arms folded, smiling.

"And then?"

"The others came. They buried their companion. We skinned the steetmoy and rode back to camp."

"And then? And then? And then?"

"Who are you? Why are you asking me this?"

Dekkeret had a flashing view of himself beneath the scavenger's fanged snout.

Barjazid said, "You were ashamed?"

"Of course. I put the pleasures of my sport ahead of a human life."

"You had no way of knowing she was injured."

"I sensed it. I saw it, but I didn't let myself see it, do you understand? I knew she was hurt. I kept on going."

"Who cared?"

"I cared."

"Did her tribesmen seem to care?"

"I cared."

"And so? And so? And so?"

"It mattered to me. Other things matter to them."

"You felt guilty?"

"Of course."

"You *are* guilty. Of youth, of foolishness, of naïvete."

"And are you my judge?"

"Of course I am," said Barjazid. "See my face?" He tugged at his seamed weatherbeaten jowls, pulled and twisted until his leathery desert-tanned skin began to split, and the face ripped away like a mask, revealing

THE DESERT OF STOLEN DREAMS

another face beneath, a hideous ironic distorted face twisted with convulsive mocking laughter, and the other face was Dekkeret's own.

XI

IN THAT MOMENT Dekkeret experienced a sensation as of a bright needle of piercing light driving downward through the roof of his skull. It was the most intense pain he had ever known, a sudden intolerable spike of racking anguish that burned through his brain with monstrous force. It lit a flare in his consciousness by whose baleful light he saw himself grimly illuminated, fool, romantic, boy, sole inventor of a drama about which no one else cared, inventing a tragedy that had an audience of one, seeking purgation for a sin without context, which was no sin at all except perhaps the sin of self-indulgence. In the midst of his agony Dekkeret heard a great gong tolling far away and the dry rasping sound of Barjazid's demonic laughter; then with a sudden wrenching twist he pulled free of sleep and rolled over, quivering, shaken, still afflicted by the lancing thrust of the pain, although it was beginning to fade as the last bonds of sleep dropped from him.

He struggled to rise and found himself enveloped in thick musky fur, as if the steetmoy had seized him and were crushing him against its breast. Powerful arms gripped him—*four* arms, he realized, and as Dekkeret completed the journey up out of dreams he understood that he was in the embrace of the giant Skandar woman, Khaymak Gran. Probably he had been crying out in his sleep, thrashing and flailing about, and as he scrambled to his feet she had decided he was off on another sleepwalking excursion and was determined to prevent him from going. She was hugging him with rib-cracking force.

"It's all right," he muttered, tight against her heavy gray pelt. "I'm awake! I'm not going anywhere!"

Still she clung to him.

"You're—hurting—me—"

He fought for breath. In her great awkward solicitousness she was apt to kill him with motherly kindness. Dekkeret pushed, even kicked, twisted, hammered at her with his head. Somehow as he wriggled in her grasp he threw her off balance, and they toppled together, she beneath him; at the last moment her arms opened, allowing Dekkeret to spin away. He landed on both knees and crouched where he fell, aching in a dozen places and befuddled by all that had happened in the last few moments. But not so befuddled that when he stood up he failed to see Barjazid, on the far side of the floater, hastily removing some sort of mechanism from his forehead, some slender crownlike circlet, and attempting to conceal it in a compartment of the floater.

"What was that?" Dekkeret demanded.

Barjazid looked uncharacteristically flustered. "Nothing. A toy, only."

"Let me see."

Barjazid seemed to signal. Out of the corner of his eye Dekkeret saw Khaymak Gran getting to her feet and beginning to reach for him again, but before the ponderous Skandar could manage it Dekkeret had skipped out of the way and darted around the floater to Barjazid's side. The little man was still busy with his intricate bit of machinery. Dekkeret, looming over him as the Skandar had loomed over Dekkeret, swiftly caught Barjazid's hand and yanked it up behind his back. Then he plucked the mechanism from its storage case and examined it.

Everyone was awake now. The Vroon stared goggle-eyed at what was going on; and young Dinitak, producing a knife that was not much unlike the one in Dekkeret's dream, glared up at him and said, "Let go of my father."

Dekkeret swung Barjazid around to serve as a shield.

"Tell your son to put that blade away," he said.

Barjazid was silent.

Dekkeret said, "He drops the blade or I smash this thing in my hand. Which?"

Barjazid gave the order in a low growling tone. Dinitak pitched the knife into the sand almost at Dekkeret's feet, and Dekkeret, taking one step forward, pulled it to him and kicked it behind him. He dangled the mechanism in Barjazid's face: a thing of gold and crystal and ivory, elaborately fashioned, with mysterious wires and connections.

"What is this?" Dekkeret said.

"I told you. A toy. Please—give it to me, before you break it."

"What is the function of this toy?"

"It amuses me while I sleep," said Barjazid hoarsely.

"In what way?"

THE DESERT OF STOLEN DREAMS

"It enhances my dreams and makes them more interesting."

Dekkeret took a closer look at it. "If I put it on, will it enhance my dreams?"

"It will only harm you, Initiate."

"Tell me what it does for you."

"That is very hard to describe," Barjazid said.

"Work at it. Strive to find the words. How did you become a figure in my dream, Barjazid? You had no business being in that particular dream."

The little man shrugged. He said uncomfortably, "Was I in your dream? How would I know what was happening in your dream? Anyone can be in anybody's dream."

"I think this machine may have helped put you there. And may have helped you know what I was dreaming."

Barjazid responded only with glum silence.

Dekkeret said, "Describe the workings of this machine, or I'll grind it to scrap in my hand."

"Please—"

Dekkeret's thick strong fingers closed on one of the most fragile-looking parts of the device. Barjazid sucked in his breath; his body went taut in Dekkeret's grip.

"Well?" Dekkeret said.

"Your guess is right. It—it lets me enter sleeping minds."

"Truly? Where did you get such a thing?"

"My own invention. A notion that I have been perfecting over a number of years."

"Like the machines of the Lady of the Isle?"

"Different. More powerful. She can only speak to minds; I can read dreams, control the shape of them, take command of a person's sleeping mind to a great degree."

"And this device is entirely of your own making. Not stolen from the Isle."

"Mine alone," Barjazid murmured.

A torrent of rage surged through Dekkeret. For an instant he wanted to crush Barjazid's machine in one quick squeeze and then to grind Barjazid himself to pulp. Remembering all of Barjazid's half-truths and evasions and outright lies, thinking of the way Barjazid had meddled in his dreams, how he had wantonly distorted and transformed the healing rest Dekkeret so sorely needed, how he had interposed layers of fears and torments and uncertainties into that Lady-sent gift, his own true blissful rest, Dekkeret felt an almost murderous fury at having been invaded and manipulated in this fashion. His heart pounded, his throat went dry, his vision blurred. His hand tightened on Barjazid's bent arm until the small man whimpered and mewed. Harder—harder—break it off—

No.

Dekkeret reached some inner peak of anger and held himself there a moment, and then let himself descend the farther slope toward tranquility. Gradually he regained his steadiness, caught his breath, eased the drumming in his chest. He held tight to Barjazid until he felt altogether calm. Then he released the little man and shoved him forward against the floater. Barjazid staggered and clung to the vehicle's curving side. All color seemed to have drained from his face. Tenderly

THE DESERT OF STOLEN DREAMS

he rubbed his bruised arm, and glanced up at Dekkeret with an expression that seemed to be compounded equally of terror and pain and resentment.

With care Dekkeret studied the curious instrument, gently rubbing the tips of his fingers over its elegant and complicated parts. Then he moved as if to put it on his own forehead.

Barjazid gasped. "Don't!"

"What will happen? Will I damage it?"

"You will. And yourself as well."

Dekkeret nodded. He doubted that Barjazid was bluffing, but he did not care to find out.

After a moment he said, "There are no Shapeshifter dream-stealers hiding in this desert, is that right?"

"That is so," Barjazid whispered.

"Only you, secretly experimenting on the minds of other travelers. Yes?"

"Yes."

"And causing them to die."

"No," Barjazid said. "I intended no deaths. If they died, it was because they became alarmed, became confused, because they panicked and ran off into dangerous places—because they began to wander in their sleep, as you did—"

"But they died because you had meddled in their minds."

"Who can be sure of that? Some died, some did not. I had no desire to have anyone perish. Remember, when *you* wandered away, we searched diligently for you."

"I had hired you to guide and protect me," said Dekkeret. "The others were innocent strangers whom you preyed on from afar, is that not so?"

Barjazid was silent.

"You knew that people were dying as a direct result of your experiments, and you went on experimenting."

Barjazid shrugged.

"How long were you doing this?"

"Several years."

"And for what reason?"

Barjazid looked toward the side. "I told you once, I would never answer a question of that sort."

"And if I break your machine?"

"You will break it anyway."

"Not so," Dekkeret replied. "Here. Take it."

"*What?*"

Dekkeret extended his hand, with the dream-machine resting on his palm. "Go on. Take it. Put it away. I don't want the thing."

"You're not going to kill me?" Barjazid said in wonder.

"Am I your judge? If I catch you using that device on me again, I'll kill you sure enough. But otherwise, no. Killing is not my sport. I have one sin on my soul as it is. And I need you to get me back to Tolaghai, or have you forgotten that?"

"Of course. Of course." Barjazid looked astounded at Dekkeret's mercy.

Dekkeret said, "Why would I want to kill you?"

"For entering your mind—for interfering with your dreams—"

"Ah."

"For putting your life at risk on the desert."

"That too."

"And yet you aren't eager for vengeance?"

Dekkeret shook his head. "You took great liberties with my soul, and that angered me, but the anger is past and done with. I won't punish you. We've had a transaction, you and I, and I've had my money's worth from you, and this thing of yours has been of value to me." He leaned close and said in a low, earnest voice, "I came to Suvrael full of doubt and confusion and guilt, looking to purge myself through physical suffering. That was foolishness. Physical suffering makes the body uncomfortable and strengthens the will, but it does little for the wounded spirit. You gave me something else, you and your mind-meddling toy. You tormented me in dreams and held up a mirror to my soul, and I saw myself clearly. How much of that last dream were you really able to read, Barjazid?"

"You were in a forest—in the north—"

"Yes."

"Hunting. One of your companions was injured by an animal, yes? Is that it?"

"Go on."

"And you ignored her. You continued the chase. And afterward, when you went back to see about her, it was too late, and you blamed yourself for her death. I sensed the great guilt in you. I felt the power of it radiating from you."

"Yes," Dekkeret said. "Guilt that I'll bear forever. But there's nothing that can be done for her now, is there?" An astonishing calmness had spread through him. He was not altogether sure what had happened, except that in his dream he had confronted the events of the Khyntor forest at last, and had faced the truth of what he had done there and what he had not done, had understood, in a way that he could not define in words, that it was folly to flagellate himself for all his lifetime over a single act of carelessness and unfeeling stupidity, that the moment had come to put aside all self-accusation and get on with the business of his life. The process of forgiving himself was under way. He had come to Suvrael to be purged and somehow he had accomplished that. And he owed Barjazid thanks for that favor. To Barjazid he said, "I might have saved her, or maybe not; but my mind was elsewhere, and in my foolishness I passed her by to make my kill. But wallowing in guilt is no useful means of atonement, eh, Barjazid? The dead are dead. My services must be offered to the living. Come: turn this floater and let's begin heading back toward Tolaghai."

"And what about your visit to the rangelands? What about Ghyzyn Kor?"

"A silly mission. It no longer matters, these questions of meat shortages and trade imbalances. Those problems are already solved. Take me to Tolaghai."

"And then?"

"You will come with me to Castle Mount. To demonstrate your toy before the Coronal."

"No!" Barjazid cried in horror. He looked genuinely frightened for the first time since Dekkeret had known him. "I beg you—"

"Father?" said Dinitak.

Under the midday sun the boy seemed ablaze with light. There was a wild and fiery look of pride on his face.

"Father, go with him to Castle Mount. Let him show his masters what we have here."

THE DESERT OF STOLEN DREAMS

Barjazid moistened his lips. "I fear—"

"Fear nothing. Our time is now beginning."

Dekkeret looked from one to the other, from the suddenly timid and shrunken old man to the transfigured and glowing boy. He sensed that historic things were happening, that mighty forces were shifting out of balance and into a new configuration, and this he barely comprehended, except to know that his destinies and those of these desert folk were tied in some way together; and the dream-reading machine that Barjazid had created was the thread that bound their lives.

Barjazid said huskily, "What will happen to me on Castle Mount, then?"

"I have no idea," said Dekkeret. "Perhaps they'll take your head and mount it atop Lord Ossier's Parapet. Or perhaps you'll find yourself set up on high as a Power of Majipoor. Anything might happen. How would I know?" He realized that he did not care, that he was indifferent to Barjazid's fate, that he felt no anger at all toward this seedy little tinkerer with minds, but only a kind of perverse abstract gratitude for Barjazid's having helped rid him of his own demons. "These matters are in the Coronal's hands. But one thing is certain, that you will go with me to the Mount, and this machine of yours with us. Come, now, turn this floater, take me to Tolaghai."

"It is still daytime," Barjazid muttered. "The heat of the day rages at its highest."

"We'll manage. Come: get us moving, and fast! We have a ship to catch in Tolaghai, and there's a woman in that city I want to see again, before we set sail!"

XII

HESE EVENTS happened in the young manhood of him who was to become the Coronal Lord Dekkeret in the pontificate of Prestimion. And it was the boy Dinitak Barjazid who would be the first to rule in Suvrael over the minds of all the sleepers of Majipoor, with the title of King of Dreams.

THE DESERT OF STOLEN DREAMS
by Robert Silverberg

Illustrated by Stephen E. Fabian

First published in this form in May, 1981 and limited to 1000 copies, of which 220 were specially bound and signed by the author; of these 200 copies were numbered and 20 copies were marked "Presentation Copy". The text was set in Mallard II, a typeface design based on Hermann Zapf's Melior, on a Compugraphic EditWriter 7500 by Jeff Levin of Pendragon Graphics, Portland, Oregon. Halftone negatives by Circus Lithograph, San Francisco, California. Text paper is 60# Warrens "66", an acid-free paper with extended shelf life. This book was printed, smyth sewn and casebound by Braun-Brumfield, Inc., Ann Arbor, Michigan, in connection with Paul de Fremery & Co., San Francisco, California.